DOUBLE TROUBLE
AT
THE ROOMS

WRITTEN BY LISA DALRYMPLE
ILLUSTRATIONS BY ELIZABETH PRATT-WHEELER

for Sophie!

Happy Reading ☺

Elizabeth Pratt-Wheeler

Tuckamore Books
a Creative Publishers imprint
St. John's, Newfoundland and Labrador
2016

We gratefully acknowledge the financial support of the Canada Council for the Arts, the Government of Canada through the Canada Book Fund (CBF), and the Government of Newfoundland and Labrador through the Department of Business, Tourism, Culture and Rural Development for our publishing program.

Cover Design and Illustrations by Elizabeth Pratt
Printed on acid-free paper

Published by
TUCKAMORE BOOKS
an imprint of CREATIVE BOOK PUBLISHING
a Transcontinental Inc. associated company
P.O. Box 8660, Stn. A
St. John's, Newfoundland and Labrador A1B 3T7

Printed in Canada by:
TRANSCONTINENTAL INC.

Library and Archives Canada Cataloguing in Publication

Dalrymple, Lisa, author
Double trouble at the Rooms / written by Lisa Dalrymple ; illustrated by Elizabeth Pratt-Wheeler.

ISBN 978-1-77103-079-3 (paperback)

I. Pratt, Elizabeth, 1985-, illustrator II. Title.

PS8607.A47D68 2016   jC813'.6   C2016-901101-1

For Natalie Sage–where Bear's story began.
And, of course, for Marc.

– LISA

For Thomas. Thank you for being my inspiration.
I love you always in all ways.

– ELIZABETH

Nat is excited. Her class is delighted.
Everyone, even her bear, is invited

to tour the museum perched up on the hill.
Mum mentions it's really quite roomy but still....

she thinks that they probably won't let Bear stay.
"No place has the space for his polar bear play."
Bear sniffles a bit, so Nat makes a mug
of cocoa with fish sticks and gives him a hug.

Bear bounces and bumps into St. John's town.
Past jelly bean houses. First up and then dOWwn

Hill O' Chips and around Cabot Tower,
singing *99 Bottles of Pop* for an hour!

Nat reads the sign and watches Bear grin.
If this is The Rooms, then they must let him in!

Mr. Scott goes to warn them as Bear starts to run,
"No running! No rushing! No pushing! Have fun!"

Up hundreds of stairs, then a hundred stairs more,
and up to the third-level gallery floor,

where Nat can see foxes, an owl and a hare.
She's grinning. The Rooms *does* have room for a bear!

A black bear named Peter. He's prowling and proud.
Bear wants to play, but *Is Peter allowed?*
The guard says, "Of course not. He's just a display."
But Peter's mouth twitches. His twinkling eyes say,

Don't listen to Bill, b'y. I'll show you around.
He jumps from his rock with a thundering sound.
Bill fumbles his coffee. It falls to the floor,
as Peter and Bear quickly roar out the door.

Nat's happy to see that Bear's found a new friend,
but worried about how this story might end.
If Bear gets sent home, then what would Mum do?
And what if this new bear gets sent with him too?

She laces her sneakers. She chases those bears
up millions, bazillions, kajillions more stairs.

Wait! Why are there jelly bean houses in here?
And while she's befuddled, both bears disappear.
These jelly bean houses are better outside!
There's too many places those stinkers can hide.

There! In a doorway, Nat sees a furred face.

No running. Of course not! (Except in this case.)

Nat follows those fur balls. And Bill follows her.

Now Mr. Scott's caught in a panda fur blur.

"This is your very last warning," he booms.

But what are these statues on view at The Rooms?

Mi'kmaq and Inuit, Irish and French,
hunters and fishermen, ladies and gents.

Bill looks them over. "No Peter," he sighs.
But Nat recognizes that dancing girl's eyes.

She whistles to warn them. She waves in alarm.

The bears leave their partners. Each one takes her arm.

They're fleeing and flying and fumbling too.

Next thing, Nat's up in a birch bark canoe,

high in the rafters, above all those stairs,
squashed between doublesome, troublesome bears.
Nat bellows, "Land ho!" and the bears give a roar.
They rock the boat forward. It points to the floor.

They lean on each landing. They zag and they zig,
with Nat hanging out and Bear losing his wig.
Bill hollers, "Look out!" Mr. Scott's almost wailing.
The boat smashes into the bottommost railing.

The front door is looming. It's propped open wide.
Bear glances at Peter and points him outside.
He's free to skedaddle. But Peter says no.
He's had so much fun. Now he hopes Bear won't go.

Nat reaches out and she touches Bear's fur.
She looks at her friend, and her friend looks at her.
She whispers, "We finally found where you fit.
Just one little thing: Bill won't like this a bit."

Oh no! He's behind them.

"Hey, wait up for me!
You left and I'm lonely in Gallery Three."

Bear falters. His eyes say, *I **would** like to stay.*
"Don't worry," Nat tells him. "You know I'll come play."
Bear gives her a hug, before turning to run,
as Nat calls, "No fighting. No biting. Have fun!"

My first visit back to see Bear!

October 12

Trying to catch the twinkly bugs in the café.

May 21

Bear pretending to squish Cabot Tower. He's so silly!

June 16

Lisa loves camping with her husband and their three kids. In real life, they know it's best not to invite the bears to play!

Elizabeth lives with her husband and her busy boy who were both an inspiration for the silliness in this book.